Meli's Journal
Joy Beach

by

Melissa Anne Poteat

Walk upright and harm none.

George W Stevenson

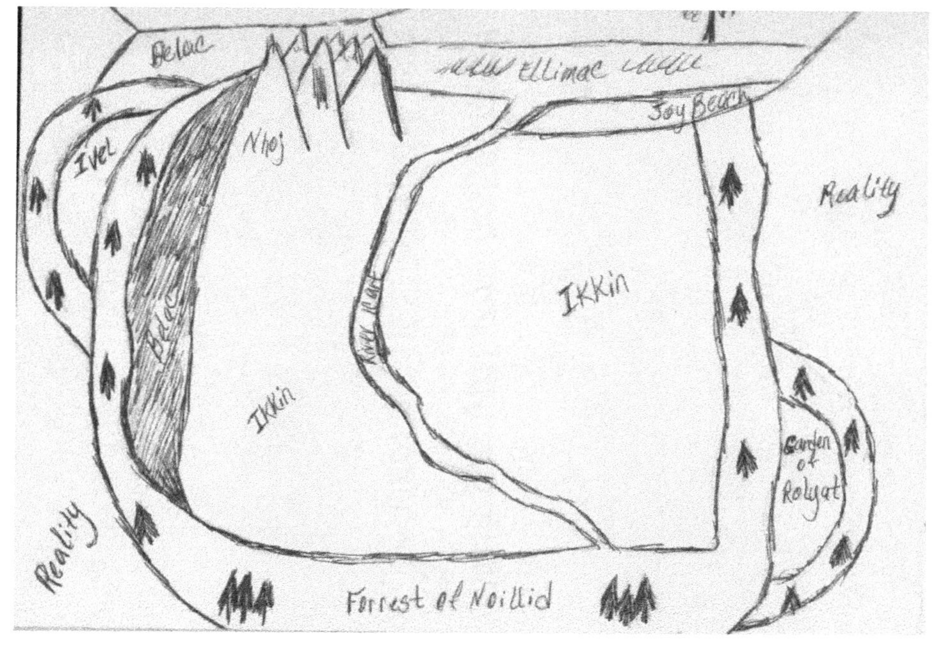
Belac
Ellimac
Joy Beach
Ivel
Reality
Ikkin
Ikkin
Garden of Rolyat
Reality
Forrest of Noillid

Preface

Traveling to many different lands, Melinda took time to jot down different things that she saw at different occasions that she would get to experience. She felt that this would be a good way of documenting what she saw. She never intended anyone of reading her journals, but it was just something that she enjoyed doing after her adventures.

Meli found not only adventure at Joy Beach, she also found life. From sea turtles, to sand castles she found a land where happiness was in every part. This land of salt and sand gave her a new perspective on making the best with whatever you are given.

January

Today Beast and I found ourselves on the shorelines of Ellimac. This beach was sure to be a Joy to us both; at least that is what I thought until I was talking to Beast about the salty air and how the experts always say that is good for people who have sinus problems. I thought he was behind me until I head no response from him. When I turned to see where he was; he was no where to be seen.

I walked back to where the footprints in the sand were only mine. They led me to a huge sink hole in the sand. There was my beloved friend with his head sticking out of it. He didn't bark indicating anything was wrong, he was just stuck in the sand. The white sands had engulfed him up to his chin.

As I dug him out I told him that this was not a good way to start the day off. I don't think he really minded me ribbing him about it. I think he was just happy to be freed from the sand. Silly pup!

Once he was out and running around again, I warned him that too many snacks would cause this to happen. I was just joking with him, but this did stir cautions signs in my head that we would have to be careful where we stepped.

February

Shells galore were what Beast and I found today at Joy Beach! The waters of Ellimac had washed them up to the shore. There were no animals inside of them. I told Beast that maybe they had all found new homes...on the same day?

Beast sniffed around the array of colored shells. They were very beautiful. Not like the shells one might find in reality. Oh no, these shells had gem stones in them. I could not help but think that if I had a shell like these, I would not trade it in for another one.

Suddenly we heard something that sounded like a heard of horses running on an open plain. I looked around into Ikkin to see if something was coming. Then I realized that the commotion was

Coming from the water. I told Beast to get ready because what ever was getting ready to come out of the

water was going to be big. I was wrong.

One by one we saw small creatures coming from the water. Big? No. Bunches? Yes! There were thousands of naked creatures. They had not shed their homes; they were just big enough to get their homes.

Beast and I stood still so that we would not step on any of the little guys. One of the little guys crawled up Beasts' right front paw. I told him not to panic, just stay where he was at. The unshelled creature crawled up his leg, over his shoulder, across his back to the tip of his tail where Beast allowed the blond curled tail to lower towards the ground to allow the little guy to get back onto the white sands. It was quite a sight.

As the creatures entered their homes, they scurried back into the waters of Ellimac. Once they were all gone, the white sands of the beach were peaceful once again.

March

Today Beast and I walked along Joy Beach. The breeze was perfect with its salty twist. We noticed that seagulls were flying above. It was almost like they were circling prey. This unnerved me because being the only two breathing things on the beach meant they were circling us.

That's what I thought.

Beast started barking at the sands. I thought he had gone crazy until I saw that the sands were moving. Something was digging its way up to the surface. Beast and I backed towards the water until we were standing in it. I called for my sword just to be safe.

Suddenly a little head popped up out of the sand. Then another and another. I was excited when I saw *that it was baby sea turtles. They were hatching and headed to the waters.*

I told Beast to check them out. They were newborn babies. He was excited until he saw that there were thousands and they were headed towards the water; which was where we were standing. I told him to go on out into the water and make sure nothing was in the water waiting for them; predators you know.

I knew I was going to have to watch the seagulls to make sure they did not try to swoop down and eat the hatchlings. Not being able to move, because I did not want to step on any of them made my task a bit difficult.

Sure enough just as I had thought, one of the seagulls swooped towards the group of little turtles. Beast saw it coming so he barked really loud as I swung my dagger into the air wildly. The bird decided the tender young morsel was not worth the trouble of having to deal with a barking dog in the water or a crazy lady swinging a sharp object towards it, so it flew back up.

We waited to make sure all of the hatchlings were safely in the water. When the last on entered, I too went into Ellimac to make sure no underwater creatures feasted on the young one.

When Beast and I saw that the older turtles had control of the situation in keeping the wee ones safe, we went back to the beach. I was exhausted.

April

Crabs in the water
Crabs in the sand
Crabs in the memories
Of crabs in the land.

White sands were orange
From this crusty shells
Beast's paws were sore
Pinchers hurt like hell.

Kicking and screaming
I found myself be
When one big ole' crab
Got a hold of me.

Thank heavens for Beast
Coming to my rescue
He had him a feast
With the crab of blue.

What a crazy day
On that beach named Joy
Our adventure did turn
Into quite the chore.

May

Today Beast and I did clean up on the Beach. It seems that the demons of Belac have been causing havoc again.

We found several nets that had washed up from the waters of Ellimac. I have seriously got to find a way of destroying that land.

Luckily there was no life in the nets. I walked the shoreline to see if I could see any boats, but there was none to be seen. This lets me know that the demons are wising up to me visiting the lands. They must be waiting for me to leave before they come around.

After gathering up the nets, Beast and I built a fire on the beach and burnt them. I did not want any reminisce of the demons left. This was if they come back for their nets, they will see them destroyed. Maybe they will get the hint.

June

Leaping Lizards and flying fish. Well, not leaping lizards, but Beast and I did see flying fish at the beach today.

At first I just thought they were jumping out of the water until on soared over my head. They were playing with Beast after they saw that the crazy canine was going to chase them.

It was funny watching them fly just where he could not get to them. I told him that he was just jealous that he was not flying. I think he understood what I was saying because of the look he gave me. It was as if he was saying, right lady!

I do wonder sometimes what he thinks of our fantasy lands. If I had not adopted him would he have *gotten to go into someone else's fantasies? If so, would they have been as different as mine?*

I suppose some things you are not to question. Like flying fish.

July

Today Beast and I met a talking pelican on the beach. When we first met him he was not talking. He was actually dying.

Beast saw him before I did. He was laying behind one of the huge rock just this side of the water. When he saw the poor creature, he barked to let me know something was there. When I reached them, the pelican had black goo all over his face. This was covering his nostrils on the top of his beak; preventing him from getting good air flow. His eyes and beak was covered also.

I took him to the water and cleaned the goo off of him. Needless to say I was totally taken back when he started talking to me.

He told me that he had gotten into a fight with another pelican. The other pelican was rude and mean to

him so he flew into him. When he did the other pelican turned into a black goo mess. He was not able to get the goo off of him so he figured he was going to die.

He thanked me for cleaning him up and saving his life. I asked him if he realized he had battled a demon. He told me that if that was the case, it made sense because he had never met a pelican that he did not get along with. That was why he did not understand why the other pelican seemed to be looking for a fight.

I was happy that the pelican was able to defeat the demon, but this did not ease my mind that the demons are still on the move. Looks like Beast and I are going to have to pick up our paces.

August

Treasures come in different forms in reality and in fantasy. A lot of people think in reality that treasure means money, silver, gold, or precious gems. To me treasures are a child's laughter or a lover's touch.

Fantasy treasure is not much different. It is in the eye of the beholder. Today we found this out on the beach.

Beast and I were walking and enjoying the sounds of the water crashing against the huge rocks. I ever took my knee high boots off just to enjoy the sand between my toes. After I stumped my toe on something sticking out of the sand, I'd wished I had kept my boots on.

With my toe throbbing, I had Beast help me dig up what ever it was *that I stumbled over. We were excited to see that it was a treasure chest.*

Once we got it out of the sand, we then had the dilemma of getting it opened.

I called for my sword. I was able to pry it open. Well, it wasn't money, gold, silver, or precious gems. This treasure was only a treasure to one, and I must say he did not need it.

Yep, this was Beast's treasure. The chest was filled with dog treats. I told him that maybe this was the beaches" way of apologizing for burying him on our first visit. He did not care why the chest was filled with treats; he just wanted to do tricks to get them; so he did.

He sat, begged, rolled over, danced, and played dead. He is such a nut case.

September

The beach was made up of sand castles today. It was quite extraordinary. I'm not sure who had made them but they were incredible.

Now I'm not talking about little sand castles made with a pale and a small toy shovel. These were huge sand castles. Beast and I were able to enter some of them. Well, it was not too long till I knew who had made them because he was inside of one that I had gone in. He startled me and made my heart skip a beat. It was Noillid!

I told him that he was very talented in his castle making. He grumbled a bit because I was there, but then after I complimented his artistic ability, he was not so grouchy.

He told me that he liked to come to the beach and make castles in the sand. It was a way of remembering

what it was like before he crossed the barrier and turned into a troll. I told him that no matter what he looked like on the outside, he was still beautiful on the inside. I also told him that someone who was not beautiful on the inside could never create such beauty; especially out of sand.

He told me that no one had ever said anything like that to him. I reminded him that I did not judge a book by its cover. I always read the pages inside before I decided whether it was a good book or not.

I had a great visit with Noillid. I think this was the first time I had ever seen him smile. It felt good thinking that I made him happy. He has helped me, even when he could have gotten hurt. Like it or not, he has a friend in me.

October

Today the beach was very calm. I sat on the white sands with my feet in the water. Yes, I took off my boots again.

Sometimes you have to do that you know. Life does not have to be battles and go, go, go all the time. Sometimes you just have to sit back, with your boots off, and relax. Sometimes it takes a day at the beach to see that.

The breeze blew, causing the palm trees in Arreis to gently bend. The waters of Ellimac rippled as the waves gently rolled upon the shore.

Beast ran around kicking the sand up with his floppy paws. I guess that is his way of relaxing.

November

Beast and I got an early start today. Way early for Joy Beach. We got there just as the sun was coming up. It was pretty spectacular watching the sun rise up from the waters of Ellimac.

I put my feet in the water to feel that it was very warm. As the sun rose, it covered the palms of Arreis. For just a couple of moments, you would never have known that there was another land there.

Going up over our heads, the sun woke the lands up. I turned to see Ikkin behind me. The field was covered with autumn colored flowers. It is pretty wild that I am at the beach watching the sunrise; Ikkin looks as if it is preparing for fall, and reality is down right cold this time of year.

Looking over at the mountains of Nhoj, I see that the peaks of the mountains are covered with snow,

And it looks as if there may be snow in the forecast for Noillid and his forest.

Belac looks as cold and black as usual, and Rolyat I am sure is preparing his grapes and roses for the cooler weather. I looked up wondering is Assilem's flying leafers are getting ready. I could not see Ivel from where I was standing, but I would not know there anyways because of its mischief.

I love all the lands, but looking back around at the waters of Ellimac, I could not think of a better place to be today.

I think the warm sun combining with the fact that Beast woke up early today made him sleepy. I sat quietly on the beach while he napped. It was a good day!

December

Snowfall is pretty much covering all of the lands today; even the beach. I think this confused Beast. He did not know if the white sands were the white sands, or if it was snow.

When we first entered the beachy area, there was snow lying around everywhere. Even the waters of Ellimac were covered. I had even joked with Beast that we could jump on the snow that was on the water and use it as a raft. He did not seem too enthused about trying it; so we didn't.

It was a good thing too. The sun started settling into the water; heating it up. The snow began to melt. Beast freaked out a little when we heard a slight sizzling sound. I told him it was just the sun settling *into the cold water. He looked at me with a confused look on his face.*

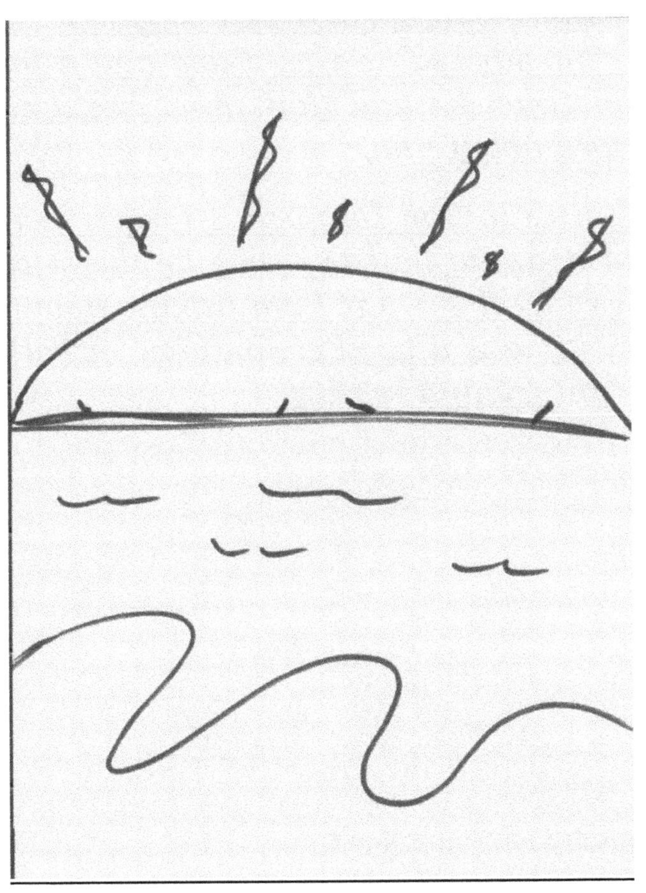

I had to remind him that we were in a fantasy land and strange things happen here. Then I remembered he was a dog and a lot of times he had that same confused look about him.

I talk to him so much; I forget he is a dog and half the time he does not even know what I am talking about. Still he is a good companion in both fantasy and reality.

From sandpits to sunsets

This beach of joy I found

The true storyteller...Uncle George

www.ingramcontent.com/pod-product-compliance
Ingram Content Group UK Ltd.
Pitfield, Milton Keynes, MK11 3LW, UK
UKHW020215250726
13967UKWH00001B/12

9 781105 715204